BARE TO DISCIPLINE

VOL. 4:
M/F SPANKING EROTICA
DISCIPLINE STORIES

C. C. Barrett

Dedication:

To my husband, I could not have done this without his support.

TABLE OF CONTENTS

DIVORCE PAPERS

BY C. C. BARRETT

Nina sat at the kitchen table. The divorce agreement, with brightly covered arrows marking where her signature should go, depressed her and made her want to cry. The prank that had started out as a way of getting attention from her husband had gone too far.

She recalled the website she had accidentally found one evening. Women just like her wrote about how they felt the need to be spanked, not only for sexual gratification but for guidance and assurance.

It took her several months before she finally confessed to her husband, Paul, of her secret desire to be a spanked wife. He seemed accommodating enough at first but as time grew, she began to feel as if something was missing. He always reminded her that they were only playing and the spankings always led to sex.

While she was at work, Paul had brought the divorce papers by when he came to mow the lawn. The papers pierced her heart as they lay on the kitchen table.

"How did it all go so wrong?" she asked herself as she began to write a letter to her husband.

Dear Paul,

I'm too embarrassed to tell you this face to face. I decided that I would try to write it down in a letter and hopefully be able to explain my feelings. These past years that we've been married have been the best of my life. I couldn't believe that it could get much better, especially when I confessed my secret desire to be spanked. I'm sure it wasn't that well kept of a secret. The DVDs and VHS tapes that included spanking scenes always turned me on as you well know.

Most people, at least openly, wouldn't understand our relationship and my need for you to express your dominance. For so long, I have felt as if I was in charge of everything, not just at work but at home as well. I can't change the way things have to be at my job but I don't want that for our home. I want you to take the lead and let me follow.

Please understand, I am not complaining or regretting what we've started. I only want to push this "experiment" further and not just for sex play. I know I act bratty sometimes and you don't understand. It's not because I want to be a bitch or treat you badly but because I want you to be authoritative and set limits. The things I've done were pushing boundaries because I need you...need you to act.

The other day, I can't remember what I had done to displease you. I was nevertheless thrilled when we were riding in the car and you told me firmly that you were going to spank me at 6:45 when we got home. I watched the clock and couldn't wait to pull into our driveway and go *upstairs to our bedroom. My stomach was doing flip flops with anxious anticipation at the expected command to prepare for a real spanking. I wanted to be punished, really chastised on the bare bottom. It didn't matter what you used, whether it was your hand, paddle, switch, belt or strap. I just wanted...needed to be disciplined.*

I knew you were tired from the drive, but I couldn't help but be disappointed when you seemed to find reasons not to spank me when we got home. Did I do something wrong? Maybe I didn't do anything wrong enough to get you to order me to bend over the edge of the bed while you yanked my shorts and panties down.

Breathlessly I waited for the time when you would take charge and walk to the drawer that contains all those instruments of punishment we have collected over the last several months.

I have signed the papers because that is what you have asked me to do. I don't want this divorce and never will.

No one is blaming you for being angry. I know what you're thinking but it's not true. I only set it up to look like I was having an affair. The roses where sent to myself, purposefully delivered when I knew you'd be home to inquire about them and "catch" me. There is no "Love, H" as the card indicated. Our next credit card statement will show the charge if you would only wait to see it.

You are probably asking yourself why I would do something to hurt you like that. Actually, I really didn't think that far ahead. I stupidly only thought you'd get angry...angry enough to send me to our bedroom for a good thrashing...a real spanking. I never thought you'd believe I wanted someone else or that you would storm out of the house like you did without saying a word. I hadn't expected you to pack your clothes and be gone before I got home from work the next day. I didn't believe you would stay away for a month, only to come by the house and mow the yard. I was totally surprised to find the divorce papers sitting on our kitchen table with your post-it note instruction *"Sign these"* attached.

Several times I tried to phone but you wouldn't take my call. I even called your mother, thinking you were staying at her house, but she didn't know where you were either. (By the way your mother says "Hello" and wants you to come see her more often.)

I'm sorry for hurting you. Please give me...us another chance. I promise I'll never ask you to spank me again.

With all my love and sincerest apology,

Nina

Nina mailed the divorce papers and her letter the next morning.

***

Paul was surprised and a bit depressed when he got a call from his lawyer's office a few days later. The message was clear enough. His wife had returned the papers but his lawyer, James Layhew, wanted him to make an appointment before filing them.

Sitting in his lawyer's office, in front of the large oak desk, Paul had to fight back the tears that threatened to cloud his vision. He couldn't believe Nina had actually signed the papers. He had spent the last few weeks, living in a motel, trying to convince himself that it was some kind of joke. Nina wouldn't cheat on me, he told himself. But her favorite flowers, pink roses, and the heartfelt card kept him up at night. His pride kept him from taking her calls.

Who the hell is "H" anyway, he'd wondered. He couldn't think of a single one of their friends whose name began with the letter "H". Probably someone from work, he finally concluded.

"As my secretary told you on the phone Paul, your wife returned the divorce documents," Mr. Layhew said.

"Did she refuse to sign them? Is that why you called me in?" Paul asked, hope creeping into his voice.

"No, she signed them correctly," the attorney confirmed, looking at the documents on his desk.

The look of misery on Paul's face made James smile. He knew he had done the right thing by insisting his client come to see him.

"She also sent a letter...its addressed to you," James said, handing Paul the letter.

Paul took the letter in trembling hands. With a deep breath, he began reading it.

Taking a call in his conference room, James left Paul alone to absorb all that Nina had written.

When James returned, he found Paul smiling.

11

"What would you like me to do?" Mr. Layhew asked, taking his seat across from Paul.

"This letter..." Paul held up his wife's note with some embarrassment, sure his attorney had also read it.

"I can file these tomorrow," James assured him. "Or..."

"Or what?" Paul asked quickly, grabbing onto the tiniest idea of hope.

"Or you can go back to your wife...give her what she wants," the lawyer said matter-of-factly.

His words took Paul by surprise.

"Perhaps if more marriages today were like the one your wife says she wants...I'd be out of the divorce business," James said, his wrinkled face spreading into a wide smile.

***

Nina was in the kitchen, heating leftovers from the previous night. She had no appetite but knew she had to eat or risk illness. She heard such a commotion at the front door that she almost dropped the plate as she took it out of the microwave.

"What the hell is going on?" she asked crossly, leaving the kitchen and going into the front foyer.

She stopped dead in her tracks. Paul was holding the storm door open with his shoulder while trying to maneuver three large suitcases through the heavy front door. She stood frozen, partially hoping he had returned and somewhat afraid he was only back to refill the luggage.

He leaned his back against the front door and made it shut with a loud bang, proud of himself for bringing in his belongs in one trip. He addressed Nina, who was still staring dumbly at him from the foyer.

"What's the meaning of these?" he asked harshly, waving the divorce papers at her.

"I signed them, like YOU wanted," she retorted, confused by his abrupt tone.

"I DIDN'T WANT THIS," he said, letting the anger from her flower delivery deception wash over him.

"I...I..." she was stunned by his confession as a look of relief spread across her face.

"You truly wanted to be disciplined?" he asked, now pulling out her letter from his coat pocket.

Nina felt ashamed of her actions and couldn't look him in the eyes. She merely nodded her head.

"That's 'Yes sir'," he said tightly.

Not waiting for a reply, he grabbed her hand and led her to the kitchen.

"Yes sir," she answered, stunned by his dominance.

"You want discipline, well I'm just the man to give it to you," Paul said, taking a chair from the table.

Without any warning, he pulled Nina over his knee and began to swat her jean clad behind.

Nina was shocked at how quickly his hand spanking began to hurt even through her thick jeans.

"Please Paul. It hurts," she said, beginning to wiggle her backside.

Abruptly Paul stopped spanking and put her on her feet.

"A REAL spanking is supposed to hurt. Now get me the pizza spatula," he ordered, pointing to the drawer.

"But...but..." Nina stammered.

"You wanted this, now do as I say or you can expect another spanking for disobedience," he said matter-of-factly.

Nina fished through the drawer and withdrew the quarter inch thick pizza paddle that had come with their pizza stone. For the first time, she noticed that it was five inches wide.

With a shiver running up her spine, she handed the paddle to Paul.

"Take down your jeans and panties," he said sternly, watching the play of emotions that crossed her face.

Her fingers felt thick and clumsy as she unbuttoned and unzipped her jeans. There was a brief hesitation as she looked at the paddle in her husband's hand.

"Down," was all he said, before she wiggled her hips, sliding her jeans and panties down to her ankles.

"OVER," he commanded, waving the paddle across his lap.

Nina took a deep breath and placed herself submissively over his lap. She grabbed the chair's legs for support as he lifted her bottom higher. Her naked ass cheeks clenched involuntarily with anticipation.

The first crack of the paddle sounded especially loud to her ears. The sting that followed was shocking. This was no play spanking, she realized immediately as another, even harder, swat of the wooden implement struck her bare heinie.

"This spanking is for signing the divorce papers," he scolded, laying three more strikes of the paddle to the underside of her pink buns.

"OOOHHH! OOOHHH!" she wailed. "But I thought you...wanted me to," she confessed.

"You were WRONG!" he said, paddling her fast and furious, thinking of all the sleepless nights he'd spent in the motel.

"Please, ppplease I'm sssooorrry!" she cried rocking back and forth, trying to dislodge herself from his lap.

"Be still!" he said, paddling her harder.

"Stop, stop, please stop!" she pleaded, her backside hurting so much she could barely speak.

"I decide when your spanking is over," he informed her as he continued to paddle her reddened ass cheeks.

"Toothpicks, TOOTHPICKS!" she cried out.

Paul recognized their safe word but continued to lay the wood to her bouncing bum.

"Not this time," he assured her. "This is a punishment spanking sweetheart. There are no safe words when you are being disciplined."

Nina's pitiful cries turned to heart wrenching sobs as her paddling continued for another full minute.

When he was finally finished, Paul sent his wife to stand facing the corner by the refrigerator with her jeans and panties still around her ankles.

"Do you still think you want REAL spankings?" he asked, looking at her reddish purple ass that was sure to have bruises tomorrow.

Nina turned just her head to look at her husband. It hurt...ALOT, she recognized before answering. But he is right, she thought as she nodded her head. She should never have signed the divorce papers.

"Yes sir or No sir?" Paul asked sharply.

"Yes sir," she admitted.

Paul seemed pleased with her answer. "Good, then you'll understand why this next spanking is going to be with my belt," he said, standing.

Nina gasped at his words.

"I'm going to punish you for the deception with the flower delivery," he stated.

"Oh," was all Nina could think to say.

She heard the jingle of his belt buckle as it came undone.

"I'm not sure one whipping is going to be enough after the month you put us through," he warned, doubling his belt. "Now put your hands in the seat of this chair!" he commanded.

The first two lashes with the belt didn't hurt as much as Nina had expected, but the remaining eight almost made her legs buckle under her. Paul had never laid into her so hard before.

"I think that will suffice...for now," he announced.

"For now...there's more to come?" Nina asked as she reached behind her and felt the large puffy welts that the belt had raised on her tender ass.

"That will be my decision, but for now hold your position!" Paul ordered as he lowered his trousers to reveal his rock hard cock. "After all, it's been a month since I've had any."

Paul entered her from behind and kneaded the punished flesh of Nina's ass as his balls swung forward and slapped against her pussy. Though the pain was intense, she pumped backward against his every stroke. This is an unexpected finale to such a harsh whipping, Nina thought. She climaxed wildly just before Paul withdrew his pulsating dick and shot a huge load of cum onto her ass. Reaching behind her, she caressed her sore bottom and rubbed his spunk into it like a creamy lotion.

"I love you baby, that's just what I needed," Nina said with a smile.

CYBERSPANK

BY C. C. BARRETT

Jenny sat in front of the monitor as the bluish light shone on her face, casting shadows across her bedroom wall. It was 3:37 A.M. according to the clock at the bottom corner of the screen. With a click of her mouse, the website opened. A friend from work had told her about the site and after tossing and turning in bed for several hours, Jenny finally got up and turned on her computer.

She read the advertisement and almost laughed. She remembered her friend, Jeff, reading the dating site's media blitz out loud from his cubicle next to hers. He had her rolling on the floor with tears of laughter when he stood in the walkway between their cubicles and acted out an imaginary ditzy blonde's profile.

"Hi, I'm Bambi and I like teeny bikinis and romantic walks on the beach," Jeff had said in a high pitched voice, wagging his backside as he swayed down the aisle.

Jenny smiled at the memory of Jeff making fun of the dating site. Her smile faded as she looked around her empty apartment. The loneliness made her ache inside.

Turning her attention back to the computer, she took a deep breath and with a few clicks of the mouse, she found the login page. Searching through her wallet she pulled out her credit card and began the lengthy registration process.

By 5 AM she had completed all the in-depth questions. The bright orange warning *"BE COMPLETELY HONEST"* flashed every so often, which encouraged her to go back and change some answers so they were more truthful.

"I'll never find what I'm looking for," she grumbled discouragingly before pressing the "Submit" button.

Looking at the clock by her nightstand, she climbed back into bed. Pulling the covers up, she hoped to squeeze some rest out of the remaining hour before she had to get ready for work.

***

At her desk, Jenny peeked over her cubicle to see if anyone was walking nearby. Assured that all her co-workers were busy with their duties, she logged into the dating website. While getting ready for work, she had kept thinking about her answers to the very personal questions on her registration.

She didn't know what made her disclose that she liked dominant men, that she liked to be spanked during sex or fantasized about receiving a real spanking. Any guy who reads that will think I'm a freak or some man hater trying to set him up for assault, she thought miserably.

Scanning her page she was disheartened immediately when the words "*Profile building in progress*" appeared in red, not allowing her to access her account yet.

"I should never have written that," she chided herself, thinking of all the politically incorrect answers she'd written.

"Did you say something?" Jeff asked as he hovered down at her from over the top of her cubicle.

Quickly minimizing the page, she blushed intensely.

"Nothing important," she assured him. "I may have set women's lib back a century," she grumbled under her breath.

"I brought you this," Jeff said, handing her a cup of coffee. "You look tired this morning."

All day Jenny kept trying to get into her profile on the dating site and each time she was denied access while the site was processing her registration.

After trying one last time before gathering her belongings to leave for the day, she cursed under her breath as the familiar red lettered "*access denied*" notice appeared.

"Up for pizza and beer?" Jeff asked from behind her.

Startled, Jenny quickly shut off her computer and nodded. Turning to face him, she looked at Jeff's face and tried to determine if he had seen what was on her computer screen.

***

Friday evening started out as usual, at the pizzeria a block from work. After a few beers, Jenny felt more relaxed and stopped worrying about the dating site. After all, my real name is protected; I'm only known by my username, "BOTMUP", she rationalized.

Jeff and Jenny were joined by a few other co-workers at first but were sitting alone together by the third pitcher of beer.

Jenny gave Jeff a goofy smile as she nibbled on her pizza crust. She was a bit tipsy but it didn't bother her. Jeff was her friend and she'd always been able to count on him.

They had met at work three years ago. Jeff had brought her to this very pizza joint on the Friday after her first week at the company. Since then it had become a tradition. Sometimes they were joined by others from work and sometimes it was just the two of them.

It had not concerned Jenny before that every Friday night since then had been spent at the same restaurant. It never bothered her until last week when someone mentioned that she didn't seem to have anything better to do on a Friday night than spend time with co-workers. Jenny laughed off the comment at first, but during the night when she was alone it began to haunt her every thought.

Her social life had definitely taken a downward turn in the last few years. Most of the good guys must already be taken, she assumed. Jenny wasn't into the bar scene and would rather stay home and watch television. Other than the men at the office and the doorman at her apartment building, she didn't take a lot of opportunities to meet someone of the opposite sex.

Jenny didn't want to think of herself as desperate but at thirty-two she decided to avail herself to the trendy matchmaking tool on the internet.

Even as a little girl, she dreamed of being a stay-at-home mother with a bunch of children and a husband she adored. Jenny never considered herself to be a leader. She would be content with a husband who would take the initiative and wouldn't be afraid to correct her with a real spanking when she needed it.

Jenny had tried to find a man who wasn't brow beaten or emasculated by today's aggressive women.

She secretively liked it when men held the door for her or paid for her meal when they were on a date.

"I'm just old fashion I guess," Jenny said with a heavy sigh before she finished the last of her beer.

She hiccupped and realized she had actually said the words aloud. She wondered what else she had vocalized.

Jeff was watching her intently from across the table. His inebriated companion began to giggle out of nervousness.

"I think I should take you home," Jeff stated, motioning for the waitress.

"I'm fine, really. I...I...oops I forgot what I was going to say," Jenny laughed, her head bobbing a bit.

"Right," Jeff said stiffly as he paid the bill and helped her to her feet.

Jenny only lived a few blocks away. Jeff had been to her apartment six months ago when she needed help moving in.

The more they walked, the drunker Jenny became. By the time they got to her apartment, Jeff had to fish through her purse to find her apartment key.

With some difficulty, he helped Jenny to her bedroom only to rush her to the bathroom before she became sick. He held her hair and when the heaves had subsided, he dampened a cloth and placed it at the nap of her slender neck.

"Y...you're a good f...friend," she said to him as she hung her head back trying to get the room to stop spinning.

Jeff smiled and helped her onto the bed. Fully clothed, Jenny passed out as he pulled a blanket off a nearby chair and covered her. He sat down and watched her sleep for a while. Before dawn and after he assured himself she would be alright, he got up to go home. His hand jarred the table next to him, bringing her computer screen to life. A fluorescent green notice flashed across the monitor that said, "*MEMBERSHIP ACCEPTED*".

***

Monday brought a mountain of work, which piled up on Jenny's desk, along with a cold drizzling rain that matched her mood. All weekend she kept checking the dating site for a match and was disappointed each time. No one appeared to have her same interests. Seated at her desk, she felt more depressed than she had before signing up. She was thinking about cancelling her membership before the free trial period ended.

Suddenly a bright blue message appeared. Username "MANXDR" was interested in corresponding with her.

"Oh my god!" she exclaimed happily before realizing she was surrounded by people in cubicles.

Looking around cautiously, she minimized the screen and began sorting through the paperwork covering her desk. She couldn't wait to get home and correspond with "MANXDR".

"You're certainly in a good mood," Jeff said as she was getting ready to go home. "I figured that extra account would bum you out."

"Not today," she said with a smile.

"How about we go…" Jeff began.

"Can't, thanks but I've got to get home," she said, cutting him off.

Jeff wrinkled his brow and watched as Jenny rushed to catch the elevator. Usually they would walk out together.

Jenny felt a little guilty as she saw the hurt look on Jeff's face as the elevator door closed. If things work out he'll understand, she thought as the car made its slow descent to the lobby.

***

The computer was on and it was almost midnight before Jenny and username "MANXDR" signed off. She wanted to continue their messaging for hours more but "MANXDR" was very firm that they both needed to get a good night's sleep. Even his writing is commanding, she thought as the dampness between her legs grew.

Before beginning to correspond with "MANXDR", Jenny had read and re-read his profile. Neither of them had posted a picture. He described himself as being an authoritarian by nature. However, he stated he was finding it hard to meet the right woman. He wrote that he's looking for someone he could be himself around and someone who wouldn't be too intimidated to submit to his will.

She scrolled back a few pages until she came to the story he wrote describing a woman at his work that day. She had been uncharacteristically rude to him. He wrote, "As I watched her round bottom swaying in retreat, I wanted to spank her right then and there".

As Jenny read the story again, her fingers found their way beneath her panties. She rubbed her clit until it became a pulsing bead. Lying back in the chair, with her legs spread apart, she teased herself. With eyes closed, Jenny pictured herself bent over her desk, elbows resting beside the keyboard, slacks and panties pushed down to her knees.

"Raise your bottom!" she imagined a strong dominant male saying, before her bare bottom was soundly slapped by his large hand.

Losing herself in her fantasy, Jenny tried not to yelp as his swats intensified. Her backside felt warm from his administrations.

"I don't believe you've learned your lesson, Jennifer," the voice said sternly, being very formal now.

She eyed the sturdy wooden ruler sticking out of her pencil holder.

"Bend over farther young lady! I'm going to blister you ass with this ruler!" the voice harshly demanded, helping her reach new heights of pleasure.

Her last thoughts before spiraling with ecstasy were of the wide ruler being forcefully applied to her bare cheeks and thighs. She envisioned thick red welts across both quivering mounds and thighs as she began to experience a wave of squirting orgasms.

***

Jenny blushed furiously as she entered her cubicle the following day. The keyboard reminded her of her fantasy.

"Did you have a good night?" Jeff asked as he poked his head up above his cubicle.

Smiling and looking down at her desk, she replied, "Yes, it was...very good."

***

"BOTMUP" and "MANXDR" continued to message back and forth each night. Jenny was tempted to check her messages during work but "MANXDR" had firmly scolded her for even thinking about shirking her work duties.

"Work and your personal life should always remain separate," he had written.

He had even threatened to blister her bottom if he caught her trying to message him during the workday.

She looked forward to going home each night and sitting at her computer. Every night for a week, during their correspondence, he never failed to tell a story about some woman at work who was disrespectful

27

or oblivious to his feelings. He would describe for Jenny in detail how, if she was his woman, he would take her home and raise welts across her ass with his belt until she saw the err of her ways.

Reading his words of punishment and correction always gave Jenny that insatiable feeling between her legs. She never denied her wanting pussy the attention of her diligent fingers while fantasizing of his dominance and chastisement.

"If only you were here," she would moan, shuttering in overwhelming orgasms.

***

Two weeks later, on a Wednesday night, Jenny turned on her computer and tried to connect with "MANXDR". When he didn't reply she stayed up until way past midnight, falling asleep at her home computer.

Thursday she couldn't wait to get home and try again. "MANXDR" wasn't responding. She hadn't realized how much she looked forward to their time together, even if it was in cyberspace. That night she cried herself to sleep and woke up the next morning with a terrible headache.

***

"Are you okay?" Jeff asked on Friday morning when Jenny came into work, looking bedraggled.

"FINE," she snapped harshly.

"This is for you," he said, reaching over the cubicle half-wall and setting a cup of coffee and donut by her keyboard.

"I...ah," she stammered, feeling a bit guilty for snapping at him. Before she could say anything in the way of thanks, he disappeared below the wall.

Jenny tried to concentrate on her work as it continued to pile up but her thoughts kept turning to "MANXDR". She missed him terribly and would give almost anything to hear from him.

She fought the urge to message him all day. As the workday was ending, she couldn't stand it one more minute and logged in. Her message to "MANXDR" was simple. "I miss you," she wrote. She was surprised when she got an immediate response.

"And I'm going to blister your ass for contacting me during your workday," he replied.

"And how do you know I didn't take the day off?" she wrote back with a smirk face icon, relieved and irritated at the same time.

"You didn't finish your donut," he wrote back.

Jenny began typing how she wasn't hungry and hadn't been for two days but stopped suddenly. She stood abruptly and looked around the room. All she could see were the tops of heads in cubicles. She suppressed the urge to run to each space and see their computer screens.

"Who are you?" she whispered under her breath.

A deep blush covered her face as she realized that someone at the office knew her secret innermost desires.

"Pizza and beer?" two of Jenny's co-workers asked as they passed by her cubicle.

"Not tonight thanks. JENNIFER and I have other plans," Jeff said decisively, giving "BOTMUP" an unwavering look.

They were the last to leave the office and Jeff had grabbed the ruler from the top drawer of Jenny's desk. A shiver of excitement went up her spine as he slapped her bottom after they entered the empty elevator.

"I'm so glad it's you," she cooed.

"We'll see how glad you are once we get to your place," he said, giving her an even harder swat with the ruler.

"Oh, I'm sure we'll both be glad," Jenny said as she leaned into Jeff while rubbing her hand down the front of his slacks, his throbbing cock responding immediately.

"Yeah, there's something I want to get straight between us," he said with a laugh. "Won't this damned elevator go any faster?" he asked with a smile.

ARRESTED

BY C. C. BARRETT

The deputy's car rolled up and stopped right beside the door marked "Prisoner Intake". Jin shuttered visibly as the deputy slammed his car door shut and came briskly around to open the back door. He helped Jin out of the back seat, her hands still in handcuffs behind her back.

Firmly but politely he ordered her and the other two girls through the door. In all her 20 years, Jin had never dreamed she would be arrested and taken to jail.

As she waited to be processed, she thought back to earlier that evening. Her lab partner at the college she attended invited her to a party. Not wanting to miss any part of the college experience, Jin gladly accepted the invitation. The frat house was across the street from the main campus. Overall she was having a great time. They played a drinking game in which those who came from places over 100 miles from a specific U.S. city had to take a drink. Because Jin was originally from China, the drinks quickly stacked up. By her fourth shot, she was beginning to feel dizzy.

The party broke up when the police arrived and requested to see identifications. Unfortunately for Jin, the legal drinking age was 21. The officer didn't care that she was only 3 months from her 21st birthday. As far as he was concerned, she had broken the law and he charged her with underage drinking. It seemed so unreal until he put handcuffs on her slender wrists and helped her into the back of his car. Jin was quickly joined by two other girls from the party. One was a freshman at the college named Lucy. The other girl, Alley, had tattoos on her neck and forearm and cursed the officer before the back door was shut.

Lucy began to cry as the cruiser pulled away from the curb. "Please, please, I won't do it again," she cried through the metal grate that separated the girls from the deputy.

"Don't waste your time," Alley said harshly.

"Oh God, my parents are going to KILL me!" Lucy wailed.

The girl with the tattoos snorted and rolled her eyes before saying, "Stop your bawling. It's no big deal."

"How do you know?" Jin asked, leaning forward to look at Alley.

"I've been arrested a lot of times before," she said, showing a tattoo on her arm. "This one I got after getting out of Juvenile Detention."

Lucy and Jin looked at Alley's arm. The barbwire that encircled her bicep was in black ink.

"Did it hurt?" Lucy asked timidly.

"Only under here," Alley said, twisting her arm to display the sensitive part underneath.

"What's going to happen to us?" Jin asked.

Before Alley could answer, the deputy barked at them to be quiet. Alley kicked the seat in front of her and stomped her foot onto the floor board before settling down into her seat.

The three sat silently as the car drove through the city streets. Jin felt sick. She didn't know if it was from the liquor or nerves. Suddenly her eyes grew large. I hope this doesn't affect my scholarship, she thought grimly.

The girls were led inside the gray block building. They were instructed to follow the blue arrow on the floor.

Alley slouched against the cold wall as they waited in line to be processed. The deputy grabbed her arm and jerked her back away from the wall.

"On the arrow!" he barked, pointing at the floor.

"Whatever," Alley spat back.

They were released from their handcuffs before being processed. Each girl was required to empty all their pockets and relinquish any wallets or purses to the woman officer. Jin watched as her house key and wallet were put inside a large envelope with her name scrawled on it.

Jin's thoughts drifted to when she had received the coveted letter from the college explaining that she had received a full scholarship covering four years of tuition and books. She would be the first in her family to attend an American college since they had transplanted from China. Her mother and father were particularly proud of her accomplishment and immediately sent telegrams and emails to all of their relatives back in Beijing.

Her brother, Chang, worked with her parents at their family restaurant. He was two years older than Jin and was happy that his little sister would have the opportunity to do more than wait on tables her entire life.

A single tear slid down Jin's face as she realized how disappointed her parents and brother will be when they discovered she has been arrested. She could hear her father's voice ringing in her ears. He had warned her to study hard and not become like those "wild American college students". She had been taught the dangers of drugs and had never touched them. She never thought an innocent frat party and a few shots of alcohol would land her in so much trouble.

"Jin Chow!" someone called out.

Jin looked up to see she was next to get her fingerprints taken. She tried to keep her hands from shaking as she allowed the officer to roll her fingers, one by one, into the black ink and then onto the form.

"Stand on that dot and face front!" she was ordered just before the flash from the camera went off.

"Turn to the right!" she heard as she tried to stop squinting in time for another flash of light.

After all three girls were processed, they were ushered into a windowless room and given orange jumpsuits and rubber sandals.

"Get undressed," the female guard instructed as she closed the door and watched the three girls disrobe.

Jin blushed with embarrassment as she unbuttoned her jeans and began lowering them to the floor.

"They smell like puke!" Alley shouted before throwing her jumpsuit at the guard.

"Put it on!" the guard ordered sternly.

"I want a CLEAN one!" Alley spat.

Lucy and Jin watched as Alley stood motionless, refusing to put on the orange jumpsuit.

"I need help in here!" the guard said, pounding on the door.

Within seconds two male officers rushed into the room.

Lucy had just zipped up her jumpsuit and was ordered to stand against the wall. Jin quickly pulled her jumpsuit up from around her knees, covering her panties and bra.

One guard stood by Lucy and Jin as they watched the other guard force Alley to bend over. Her panties were yanked to her knees. The woman guard put on a rubber glove and probed Alley's genitals before inserting a finger inside her rectum.

"You Mother-Fuckers!" Alley screamed as another finger was inserted.

Alley struggled but it was useless as the male guard held her firm. He was grinning as she continued to struggle.

"She's clean," the matron guard said, finally removing her hand.

"You gonna get dressed now?" the male guard restraining her asked.

"Not in that dirty thing!" Alley yelled back.

The matron traded places with him and she resumed a fierce hold of Alley. Her panties were still down around her knees.

The guard reached to his side and retrieved a black object hanging from his belt. It was flat on one end and made of a hard rubber. Stepping behind Alley and to the side, he drew it back and brought it across her naked ass cheeks. The loud CRACK made Jin and Lucy jump.

"Fuck you!" Alley screamed as the burning sensation began to build in her butt.

After several more hard strikes, Alley was crying and more than ready to put on the orange jumpsuit.

"You each get one phone call," the matron said, leading them to the line of payphones along a wall.

Alley rubbed her backside as she sullenly followed in line.

Lucy was handed a quarter. She looked at it and then handed it to Jin.

"I can't call my parents, I just can't!" Lucy wailed.

Jin took the quarter and walked hesitantly to the phones. There was only one person she could call. She dialed Chang's cell phone number.

Even though it was very cold in the building, sweat glistened from Jin's forehead as she listened to the constant ringing as it went unanswered. Just when she thought her call would go to his voice mail, she heard his voice.

"Hello?" Chang asked groggily.

"Chang, thank God!" Jin exclaimed.

"Jin? It's two in the morning! What's wrong?" he asked, now wide awake.

"I...I..." Jin started to cry. "I've been arrested."

"ARRESTED?" he asked in outrage.

"Please, please I need you to bring some money for bail," she begged.

"What did you do?" he asked suspiciously and then changed his mind. "Never mind, you can explain it to me on the way home."

"Please hurry," she pleaded.

***

Alley stood as soon as she saw her boyfriend behind the glass counter. He paid her bail and waited angrily for her to get dressed and collect her belongings.

"I told you not to go to that party!" he scolded, handing her a helmet as they walked out to his motorcycle.

The deputy at the night desk laughed to himself as he saw Alley's boyfriend give a quick swat to her rear end just before leaving. I bet that hurt, he thought. It was all over the station how the girl had to be punished before she would get dressed into the jail uniform.

***

Back in the holding cell, Jin and Lucy sat together holding hands. Jin wondered if Chang had decided not to come and bail her out. It was taking a long time. Jin and Lucy had arranged for the desk clerk to request the bail for both girls if Chang showed up. Lucy was too scared to call home and Jin didn't have the heart to abandon her in the cell.

Finally Jin stood up when she recognized her brother through the glass. Jin and Lucy breathed a collective sigh of relief after Chang dug in his pocket and produced the funds requested. He waited while Jin and Lucy were allowed to change and collect their personal property.

"Who is THIS?" Chang asked as Lucy followed Jin from the station.

"She's a friend of mine. I couldn't just leave her in there!" Jin explained.

"I'm Lucy," the meek, attractive girl said hesitantly.

"This is my brother Chang." Jin made the introductions with a smile.

"I suppose you need a ride home too?" Chang asked.

"Please?" Lucy asked, her eyes glistening over.

"Fine, get in," he said, shaking his head.

The three rode in silence as Chang drove toward the college dorms where Lucy lived. Jin stole glances at her big brother, trying to gauge his mood.

"I expect to be paid back!" Chang said as Lucy got out of the car in front of her dormitory.

"I will," Lucy promised before shutting the car door.

"You went to a party, didn't you?" Chang asked as they left the college campus and headed for the home they shared with their parents.

"How did you know?" Jin asked.

"You wouldn't have gotten arrested if you were studying at the library tonight like you told Father you were doing," her brother replied.

"Please don't tell Father," Jin begged.

"Too late little sister. How do you think I came up with the $200 dollars tonight? Father had to open the safe at the restaurant," said Chang.

"Oh God!" Jin rubbed her arms as a shiver came over her. "Was he very angry?" she asked.

"Wouldn't you be angry if your daughter was arrested and sitting in jail?" Chang exclaimed.

"What do you think he'll do?" Jin asked, wishing she didn't already know the answer.

"What he always does when you get into trouble," Chang said with a grimace and a shake of his head.

Jin let out a deep sigh. She could picture her mother and father waiting for her in the living room when she got home. Her father would start scolding in English but within a few minutes he would be yelling in Chinese. He always sounds harsher when he speaks in his native tongue, she thought. Sometimes her mother would try to intervene but Jin doubted she could count on that tonight.

The headlights bounced off the garage door as they pulled into the driveway. Chang got out and walked to the front door of their home. When he reached the front stoop, he turned and watched as Jin sat grimly in the front seat of the car, trying to get up the nerve to face her parents.

She had good reason to be anxious. For as long as she could remember, her parents tried to instill in their children that they were a reflection of their parents. Her actions would bring shame to her family. Her father was a proud business man and wouldn't take her arrest calmly. Getting caught in a lie was bad enough but to need bailing out of jail was much more public.

Chang waited patiently as Jin finally resigned herself to her fate and opened the car door. She walked hesitantly toward the house.

Giving her a reassuring pat on the shoulder, her brother opened the front door and they entered the brightly lit living room.

"PEEU! You stink!" her mother said as she came closer to Jin.

Her father sniffed the air and made a face before launching into his tirade. Chang was ordered to bed, leaving Jin alone with her irate parents. After ten minutes of ranting in Chinese, her father wrinkled his nose and ordered her to take a bath.

Jin hoped the time it took to get herself clean would lessen her father's anger. But the pounding on the bathroom door and his yelling for her to hurry up, dashed all hopes of his fury receding.

Wet and naked, she emerged from the bathroom and went straight into her room. She didn't bother to close the door but stood facing her bed. She could hear her parents talking in the next room but couldn't hear what they were saying.

Suddenly she heard her father enter her room. Her mother stood in the doorway. Jin shivered from fright as she was instructed to place her palms on the mattress.

Her father waved the bamboo rod in the air as if testing its durability and pliability. Satisfied with the rod, he swung back and brought the bamboo to strike sharply across the middle of her wet bare backside.

Jin cried out in pain. A thin red line appeared across both her ass cheeks. She knew to remain still, trying not to flinch as the bamboo sliced through the air for its second strike.

The pain was excruciating as another red line appeared. The dampness of her skin made the punishment even more painful. Jin sobbed openly, begging for forgiveness as her caning continued. Only after 12 straight puffy lines were covering her backside and thighs did her punishment cease.

"You not lose scholarship or you get 100 more," her father warned before leaving her to cry in pain.

***

The following Monday, Jin was surprised when Chang offered to drive her to college.

"Can you get me Lucy's phone number?" Chang asked as they pulled up at the campus.

"I'll get the money from her," Jin assured her brother.

"No it's not that," said Chang.

"Then what?" Jin asked.

Before Chang could respond, Lucy appeared on the sidewalk. She waved frantically at the siblings when she saw them.

"I don't have your money yet but my parents are wiring it to me later today," Lucy said to Chang as he rolled down the car window.

"Go out with me tonight and we can talk about it," Chang said with a grin.

Lucy blushed furiously. She hadn't been able to get the handsome Asian man out of her mind since he paid her bail and dropped her off at her dorm the other night. Her thoughts flashed back to when she was showering the smell of jail off her alabaster skin. She had stood in the shower rubbing her twat to orgasm as she imagined Chang behind her, pounding his stiff cock in and out of her welcoming body.

Lucy's thoughts returned to the present and she replied, "I'd love to."

Jin stood patiently by as her brother and Lucy made their date. The girls walked off together, arm in arm, giggling. Lucy looked back to catch Chang watching her from his car.

THE DATE

BY C. C. BARRETT

     Chang watched Lucy's plump fanny swing back and forth as she walked away toward her next class. He couldn't wait for their date later that night.

     He had been thinking about Lucy all weekend, ever since he bailed her and his sister, Jin, out of jail for underage drinking. He wondered if Lucy had gotten up the nerve to tell her parents she had been arrested.

***

     Chang listened from inside his room across the hall as Jin was disciplined by their father for breaking the law. He winced each time as the distinct crack of the bamboo rod struck her bare flesh. His little sister was being severely punished.

It had been a few years since he had felt the sting of the rod by his father's heavy hand against his bare ass but he vividly remembered the welts that lingered for days. He could hear Jin's cries mingled with his father's stern reprimand.

Chang counted 12 strokes, remembering his father always liked even numbers. He continued to listen as Jin cried herself to sleep across the hall. He felt sorry for her but knew she deserved to be punished for drinking and lying.

***

Chang envisioned the bamboo stick in his hand, Lucy's naked round ass exposed to him, as he wielded the cane. He heard her voice cry out for him to stop but he would not...could not...let her go unpunished.

Suddenly he sat up in bed. His cock was stiff and pulsating from his dream. Reaching for the hand lotion in his nightstand, he squirted some into his palm before rubbing his hard prick. The shaft moved with his fist as he pumped up and down. With his other hand, he squeezed and pulled at his balls. He continued to think of Lucy and her pretty bare rump as his cock spurted cum like a fountain.

***

When Chang brought Lucy to meet his parents after their date, he didn't expect the scene in the living room. Jin was kneeling in front of their father as he spoke rapidly in Chinese. Her head was bowed submissively as he spoke. Their mother was shaking her head in disapproval as Jin tried to explain only to be cut short by their father's angry words.

His father didn't care that Chang had brought home company and that the reprimand of his daughter was being witnessed by a guest. All that mattered was that Jin had lied to him and he would not tolerate it.

"We'll come back later," Chang said, trying to usher Lucy out the front door.

"YOU WAIT!" his father commanded.

Chang turned back around toward his father expectantly.

"You heard your sister. She say she go to study. Right?" his father asked.

Chang hated it when he was asked questions that were undoubtedly going to get Jin into trouble. He had no choice but to answer.

"Yes Father," Chang admitted sadly, looking down at his sister who was still on her knees, submissively bowed before their father.

Chang had wondered how long it would take for his parents to realize that Jin had lied the night she was caught drinking.

Knowing how smart his parents were, they probably knew right away but waited until the pain from her first punishment had subsided before commencing with another one.

"You may go," his father said, waving a hand in Chang's direction, dismissing him.

Chang turned to see that Lucy was mesmerized by the sight before her. He took a firm hold of her arm and led her out the front door and to his car.

"What's happening?" Lucy asked anxiously, peering back at the house.

"My sister, Jin, will be punished," he said.

"For what?" she asked, still looking at the house.

"For lying the night she was arrested," he stated simply.

"Did she get into trouble for drinking?" she asked hesitantly.

"Yes," Chang said icily.

He was reluctant to talk about Jin's punishment. By American standards, his traditional Asian father would be considered extremely strict and very old fashioned. Using corporal punishment on his children and sometimes on his wife was commonplace in their home.

Chang was afraid that Lucy would think his traditional family strange or weird. But he was surprised when her voice only conveyed curiosity and not judgment.

"What...I mean how was she punished for drinking?" Lucy asked shyly.

"Father gave her 12 strokes with a bamboo cane," he said, watching Lucy closely for her reaction.

Instead of the condemnation he expected, Lucy merely thought a moment before continuing her questions.

"Through her jeans?" she asked.

"No," Chang replied taking a patient breath. "My father believes in the humiliation of stripping before being punished."

"You mean she was NAKED?" Lucy asked in astonishment.

"Yes," Chang said evenly.

"What's going on now?" she asked, pointing toward the house.

"I suspect Jin will be punished for lying last Friday night about going to the library to study when she went to the party instead," he said.

"Will she get 12 strokes again?" Lucy couldn't help but ask.

"No, it will be much worse." Chang could hear his father's raised voice out in the driveway.

Lucy had never been spanked or even disciplined in her entire life. Even now she remembered how her parents responded to her arrest. It took her two days before she had finally gotten the nerve to tell them she had gotten into trouble for drinking at the frat party. But as usual, her parents tried to blame everyone else for her behavior. Instead of correcting her, they spent more time discussing which lawyer could get the matter swept under the rug.

Lucy felt confused and lonely. Like most parents, hers didn't believe in corporal punishment. Lucy's fascination with spanking was strong and she couldn't resist asking her next question.

"What's he saying?" she asked, the Chinese words filtering in through the car window.

"He is instructing Jin to go to her room. She is to remove her clothes and lay on her stomach on her bed," Chang translated.

"What's he going to do next?" she asked breathlessly.

"He will whip her," Chang said, becoming irritated.

"Oh," Lucy could only say.

"Do you want to see for yourself? I could ask my father if he will let you watch!" Chang exploded. "Then you can call the police!"

"No! I...I just wanted to know. I feel bad for her and kind of guilty," she replied hastily.

"Guilty?" Chang was surprised.

"I...I...never mind," Lucy said hanging her head. "Please take me back to my dorm."

Chang and Lucy rode in silence until they turned onto the campus. He reached beside him and took her hand in his.

"I'm sorry I got angry," he said, keeping his eyes on the road.

"No, no. I'm sorry," Lucy replied with tears in her eyes. "I shouldn't have asked all those personal questions."

"You must think my family is strange." Chang stole a quick glance in Lucy's direction.

"NO! I...I wish...never mind," Lucy said, looking down at her lap.

Chang parked just outside Lucy's dormitory. He reached for her as she was about to get out.

"Wait. What is it you wish?" he asked, taking hold of her hand again.

Lucy settled back in the passenger's seat and stared out the window for a moment. Chang could tell she was wrestling with something.

"You can tell me...anything," Chang prodded.

Lucy shook her head before saying, "You'll think I'm crazy."

"Never. You can trust me," he said encouragingly.

"I was just wondering what it was like." Her face flushed a bright red.

"You mean to be disciplined?" Change asked softly.

Lucy blushed even deeper and nodded, not able to meet his eyes.

"Real discipline hurts a lot," he said, watching her closely. When she didn't respond he continued on. "But afterwards the guilt is gone and replaced by a feeling of peace and forgiveness."

Lucy looked at Chang with tears in her eyes. "I want that," she whispered, squeezing his hand.

A stunned look came over Chang's face. He never dreamed he'd find an American woman who would allow him to have the kind of traditional relationship he had grown up with.

"Are you sure?" he asked, afraid to get his hopes up.

Tears spilled down Lucy's face as she nodded shyly. Chang took his free hand and cupped her chin, raising her face so she had to look at him.

"Tell me what you want Lucy," he said gently.

"I...I want you to...to punish me for...for drinking when I shouldn't have," she said.

"Are you sure?" Chang asked. "I promise you it will hurt," he added matter-of-factly.

"Yes," she replied, not losing eye contact with him.

Chang's cock stiffened immediately. He looked around as college students were busy walking along the sidewalk.

"We can't do this here. I'll think of a place...more private," he said, giving her hand a reassuring squeeze.

Lucy breathed a sigh of relief. He hadn't thought she was crazy or a kinky freak. He talked to her on the subject of discipline as if it were the most natural thing in the world. A smile spread across her face as her eyes shined brightly.

"When," she asked eagerly.

"Tomorrow night. I'll pick you up at eight. Be waiting right there." He pointed to the foyer of her dormitory.

"Okay," she replied happily, getting out of the car.

"And Lucy…" Chang's voice stopped her. "Wear a dress and nothing underneath," he said authoritatively.

A shiver of anticipation went up her spine upon hearing his words. Just before she closed the car door, she stopped and turned back toward Chang.

"I almost forgot," she said as she reached into her bag. "This is what I owe you for my bail." Lucy handed him a one hundred dollar bill before shutting the car door.

"Eight o'clock," he shouted after her as she skipped up the steps to her dorm.

Chang looked at the bill and then looked at Lucy's retreating form. His cock throbbed with the thought of caning her backside.

***

The next morning at the Chow's residence the family sat down for breakfast. His parents were in a good mood. Chang's father kissed his mother on the forehead before taking his usual seat at the head of the table. Jin gave a slight gasp as she sat down and then stood up abruptly.

Their mother went to get a pillow from the couch but a quick word from her husband ceased her movement.

Jin was ordered briskly to sit down on the hard wooden chair. Chang could only cringe in sympathy for his younger sibling. The rough wicker weaving in the seat irritated the welts that were certainly across his sister's backside.

"Who was that girl you brought here last night?" his mother asked abruptly after everyone was served.

"The girl from last night?" Chang repeated the question.

"Yes her," his father's eyes locked with his.

"Her name is Lucy and I think I'm going to marry her!" Chang said proudly.

His mother, father and sister gasped in unison. Chang began to laugh.

"Not for a few years but I think she's the one," he said with a smug look on his face.

His family breathed a sigh of relief as they continued to eat the remainder of their breakfast in silence.

***

Lucy tried on three different outfits before selecting the paisley printed cotton dress. Before putting on her sandals, she quickly slipped off her panties.

"Naughty naughty girl," her roommate chided with a wag of her finger, sitting up in her bed and setting her biology book aside.

Lucy blushed at having been caught getting ready as Chang had instructed. She hastily slid into her sandals and was about to leave when her roommate stopped her.

"Wait!" the roommate cried out. "You might need this," she said, reaching inside her nightstand and tossing Lucy a condom.

"Thanks," Lucy giggled as she closed the door to their room.

Chang pulled into a parking space. Lucy had been waiting in the foyer since 7:45, not wanting to be late or lose her nerve. She anxiously left the dorm and went to his car. Chang got out and opened the car door for her, nodding approvingly at her dress.

"Where are we going?" she asked nervously as he started the engine.

"To my house," he said with a wink.

"But won't your sister or parents be home?" she asked.

"My parents are at the restaurant and my sister will be studying in her room all night," he said.

He wished he could find someplace more private, but on such short notice his bedroom was the only place he could think of. Jin usually had her headphones on so she wouldn't hear them and their parents didn't get home until after nine.

The drive to the Chow's residence was faster than Lucy believed possible. She wanted to back out a hundred times during the fifteen minute drive. Chang had promised her punishment would hurt...a lot. Her palms began to sweat as they pulled into the driveway.

Chang helped her out of the car and opened the front door for her as well. She timidly walked in and looked around, assuring herself that they were alone.

"Jin is upstairs in her room," he said, pointing to the stairs.

"How do you know?" Lucy asked.

"Father will not allow her to leave the house except for her classes," Chang said, leading the way up the stairs.

"My room is this first room on the right," he said, pointing to the neat masculine room at the top of the stairs.

He left her standing in the middle of his bedroom as he disappeared down the hall to his parents' bedroom.

Lucy could see that the door to the room across the hall was closed and wondered what Jin would say if she knew Lucy was here and the purpose of her visit.

Chang walked in with a bamboo rod in his right hand. Seeing the three-quarter inch diameter limb, she suddenly felt weak in the knees and hoped her legs didn't visibly tremble.

He closed the door, making the room seem very small to Lucy. After years of growing up in the strict household, it was easy for Chang to adopt his father's mannerism and even his words, in English however.

"Why are you to be punished?" he abruptly asked Lucy.

"B...because I broke the law and drank alcohol," she said, not taking her eyes off the cane.

Pulling the chair out from behind his desk, he motioned for Lucy to bend over and place her hands in the seat.

"Don't make it hurt too badly," she pleaded as she timidly looked over her shoulder at him.

"It will hurt as much as necessary so you will remember not to ever do that again," he responded firmly. "Now raise your dress."

Lucy hesitated for a moment before tugging the material up to her waist.

"Jin received 12 with the cane for the same offense. I think that is an appropriate number," he warned.

Lucy clenched her ass cheeks together as she waited. She flinched when Chang tapped the cane slowly and gently across the middle of her exposed globes. Her instincts told her to run from the anticipated pain to come but she held fast to the seat of the chair and waited.

Chang was having a hard time controlling his libido. In his dream he didn't remember her bare bottom looking so enticing. Steeling his resolve, he swung back with the cane and brought it down with a loud "CRACK" as it made contact with Lucy's bare flesh.

The pain was sharp and much worse than Lucy had anticipated. She cried out involuntarily, forgetting that Jin was just across the hall.

"Count them," Chang commanded, taking a firmer grip on the cane.

"One," she cried out.

The next lick was delivered just below the first one.

"T...T...Two," Lucy said through trembling lips.

By the eighth whack of the cane, she was sobbing. Her backside was covered with red welts in symmetric rows across her entire bottom. Lucy made every promise she could think of that would end her punishment but nothing deterred Chang.

Two were delivered to the back of her thighs. The pain was so great she couldn't count out loud any longer. Chang counted the remaining two for her.

"Eleven," he said as he made an upward stroke to the underside of her cheeks.

Lucy wanted to reach behind her and rub the pain away but knew she had one coming. Without warning, the twelfth lick was delivered to the same spot making her howl for him to stop.

"It is over," he said, taking her in his arms. "You did very well for your first punishment," he praised her as she sobbed on his shoulder.

A knock on the door brought Lucy's head up sharply. Chang opened the door a few inches to find Jin standing on the other side. Her headphones were around her neck.

"Mother and Father are home and want you to come downstairs," Jin said. Seeing Lucy standing behind her brother, she motioned toward his guest. "Her too," she said.

Chang and Lucy descended the stairs to his waiting parents below. Lucy's eyes were puffy from crying but she had a smile on her face.

Chang awkwardly introduced her to his parents. He didn't know when they had come home or how much they had heard. It became clear to him when his father spoke to him in Chinese.

"What were the two of you doing upstairs?" his father asked. "Why has she been crying?"

"I was punishing her for drinking, like Jin," Chang replied, pointing in Jin's direction.

"Don't get me in the middle of this," Jin said in Chinese.

Jin had followed the couple down the stairs. After hearing the familiar whack of the cane, Jin had removed her headphones and laid her studies aside. It was obvious to her, as it was to their parents, what was going on in Chang's room.

Their mother, who hadn't spoken until now, turned to Lucy and in Chinese welcomed her to the family, saying that if Lucy could accept punishment from Chang, she would make him a good wife.

When Chang went to drive Lucy back to her dorm later that evening, she asked, "What did your mother say to me?"

"She is very glad to meet you," he said with a sly smile. Although his parents approved, he knew it was too soon to ask her to marry him.

THE STRANGER

BY C. C. BARRETT

Loretta wiped the sweat from her brow as the hot sun beat down. The air was dry as it blew across the prairie. Tumble weeds skittered down the street, stirring up more dust.

Unfolding the damp sheet from her basket, she longed to be wrapped in its coolness. This will be the last one today, she thought to herself as she laid the white material over the rope to dry.

She and her husband, Carl, lived a simple life. They had a small house in town. He ran the livery stable and, for extra money, she took in laundry. They made use of the space between the stables and their home for several clothes lines.

The town was beginning to boom as the railroad grew closer. She was so busy with the laundry that she could barely keep up with her housework. Carl provided the necessities but Loretta had her eye on a readymade dress at the mercantile. A few more weeks and I'll have enough money for the matching bonnet too, she thought.

She was startled when she turned to see a tall blonde man, dressed in black from his hat down to the tips of his boots. He was leaning against the stable fence, smoking a cigarette.

"Ma'am," he said, tipping his hat in her direction.

Loretta stopped short, holding her empty basket against her hip.

"Can I help you?" she asked, looking into his piercing eyes and then to the guns on each hip.

She could feel the sweat dripping down her cleavage. His eyes followed the line of moisture as it disappeared beneath her blouse. With one hand, Loretta quickly closed the material at her throat and stared at the stranger.

"Can I help you?" she asked again, a bit surlier.

"Well that depends," the stranger said with a grin, eyeing her up and down.

Loretta blushed deeply at his open stare. It felt as if he were undressing her with his eyes. She felt uncomfortable, yet excited at the same time.

"The man inside the livery said I could get my laundry done here," the stranger said, pointing toward the stable doors.

"That would be my husband, Carl," she said with irritation. "I swear that man has no sense of time!"

The man pulled out a silver dollar. The sunlight gleamed off of it. Taking an exasperated breath, Loretta held out her hand.

"You shouldn't swear," the man reproached as he handed her his saddle bags and pocketed the money. "I'll pay extra if you can mend them too," he said with a wink.

Loretta watched as the stranger swaggered down the street. She opened the saddle bags and pulled out long johns and two shirts. She looked down the street just in time to see the stranger disappear inside the saloon.

Grateful she hadn't thrown out the washing water, she went to work on the clothes. She noticed immediately that one shirt, although finely tailored, had a rip at the cuff. The clothes were covered in dust. It took longer to clean them than she anticipated.

***

Loretta looked toward the horizon and wondered how the sun had gotten to the west so fast. Just as she was taking the last of the laundry from the line, she was startled to see Carl standing behind her.

"Where's supper?" he asked placing his hands on his hips.

"Nothing is keeping you from making it!" she replied hotly, dumping her arm load of clean laundry into the basket.

"And I don't have any clean shirts," Carl complained.

"Wash them your damn self. I'm busy…" she spouted, but then shut her mouth as something caught her eye.

She froze as a silhouette of a man stood across the street. He appeared to be watching them. The smoke from his cigarette drifted around him. A chill went up her spine as she quickly went into the house.

Inside the small house, Loretta turned on her husband.

"Why don't you ever take me out anymore?" she ranted. "I clean all day and you never take me to the hotel restaurant," she complained.

"It costs money to eat there and your cooking is better," he tried to cajole her.

"Damn you Carl! We never go out!" she hollered at him.

Without saying a word, Carl walked through the little house and disappeared out the back door. A few minutes later, he was chopping wood by the wood pile as the sunlight quickly disappeared.

That night, after a meal of white beans and cornbread, Loretta sat by the fire in her rocking chair. The stranger's torn shirt lay in her lap as she occasionally glanced in her husband's direction. He was busy reading the newspaper at the table and hadn't said a word since he came in from chopping wood.

As her husband's silence drew on, her anger rose even more. Picking up the shirt, she began mending the cuff.

"I wonder what that man does to have the money to afford these fine clothes?" she said out loud.

She glanced at Carl to see his reaction. When he continued to ignore her, she began to rock furiously.

"He's handsome. Did you see those guns?" she asked, watching her husband closely.

She knew her words hit the mark when his fingers tightened around the newspaper.

"It sure makes a body wonder what a good looking man is doing around here," Loretta went on as she continued to rock in front of the fireplace. "Lord knows we lack any real men around here," she added spitefully.

Carl laid the newspaper down and turned to stare at his wife. They had only been married five years. She was the prettiest girl at the barn dance and they were wed within a month from their first introduction. But she had turned sour over the few years they'd been together. He didn't know exactly when it happened. She changed little by little over time, he suspected.

Picking up one of his dirty shirts that Loretta had carelessly slung into a corner of their bedroom, he went outside and filled a bucket with water from the pump.

The water sloshed onto the wood floor as he carried it back inside and laid it down on the table.

"Look at the mess you're making!" Loretta shrieked at him.

Ignoring her, he took the lye soap and began scrubbing his shirt until he felt it was clean and his anger had dissipated.

"You better clean that up when you're through!" she yelled as he disappeared out the back door with his sopping wet shirt, dripping a trail as he went.

He could still hear her yelling as he draped the shirt over the clothes line, hoping it would be dry by morning. It was dark and the light from the saloon down the street beckoned him. After one last glance at his home he trudged the several hundred yards to the bar.

Music was coming from the player piano as Carl stepped in, the doors swinging behind him. He took a seat on an empty barstool and ordered a beer. A poker game was going on behind him. The self-assured stranger dressed in black was placing his bet. The three other's around the table were considering the amount. Several glances went back and forth from the pile of money in the middle of the table to their cards.

The stranger never blinked as he waited patiently for his opponents to either call or fold. Carl continued to watch the game with interest and shook his head as the three lost a considerable sum to the stranger.

With nothing left, the three players, mostly cowhands, left the saloon much poorer than they had entered. The stranger, seeing Carl watching, offered a chair to him.

"No thanks Mister. Too rich for my blood," Carl wisely decided.

"Then just have a drink with me," the stranger said before ordering the bartender to bring a bottle and two glasses.

Carl left his barstool and took a seat across from the gambler. Two saloon girls sauntered up to the stranger. One was so bold to put a hand on his shoulder and whisper in his ear.

"Maybe later ladies," the man replied politely, dismissing them.

Carl watched the women retreat, wondering what it was about the man that attracted the opposite sex to him. He had to admit that the stranger was well dressed and obviously wealthy but there was something more. Carl would bet his eye teeth that the women would still clamor around the gambler if he were poor and wore simple clothes like the rest of the town folk. He wished for half the confidence the stranger evoked.

"You have troubles," the man said, looking directly at Carl before pouring them a drink.

Carl was stunned by the man's bluntness. He took the whisky and downed it quickly. A cough seized him immediately, as he wasn't accustomed to hard liquor. The gambler ignored Carl's coughing, pleased to see that the livery man wasn't accustomed to drinking.

"You got troubles with your woman," the stranger said, more as a statement than a question.

Carl nodded his head dejectedly. There was no sense in denying what the whole town already knew.

"She doesn't respect you," he added, pouring them another round. "I might be able to help you."

Their conversation continued late into the night.

***

Loretta grew irritated as she tossed and turned in bed. Carl hadn't come home and it was well past midnight. She began to wonder what it would be like to be in the arms of the handsome stranger. Her pussy began to twitch as she flicked her clit with her finger, fantasizing that the blonde stranger's tongue was licking her steamy twat. She hunched her hand furiously and a low moan escaped her lips as her juices began to flow.

When she finally heard Carl's footsteps on the front porch, she quickly turned her back and faced the bedroom wall. She could hear him undressing and the bed creaked with his weight as he lay down next to her. She was about to turn and confront him but just as his head hit the pillow he began snoring.

The next morning, making as much noise as she could, Loretta clanged the frying pan down on the woodstove. Purposefully burning the eggs, she placed Carl's breakfast on the table with a loud bang. I'll give him a piece of my mind, she decided. How dare he stay out all night, she fumed.

Carl sat down to his burnt eggs. If his head hadn't hurt so much this morning, he would ask her to cook them again. Cutting off a piece of bread, he buttered it before pouring himself a cup of strong coffee.

"Where were you last night?" Loretta launched into her tirade, her fists on her hips.

"Talking with a friend," Carl replied calmly.

"What FRIEND? A WOMAN friend?" she asked jealously. Her anger was almost uncontrollable.

Carl laughed, wincing as his head continued to pound. "No, the man that rode in yesterday. By the way he said he'll be by for his clean clothes this afternoon," Carl said.

"What would you and a successful man like that have to talk about?" Loretta asked nastily.

A smile spread across her husband's face. "Apparently a lot because we didn't finish until after midnight," he said, rising to go to the livery.

"I mended his shirt. I think I'll charge him extra since he has such fine clothes and can obviously afford it," Loretta declared.

"No need. He's already paid me," Carl said as he walked out the back door.

Loretta stared after her husband. She couldn't believe her ears. By the time she realized what he had said and opened the back door, Carl was halfway across the yard.

"Wait a damn minute!" Loretta hollered after him. "What do you mean he already paid YOU?"

Carl stopped at the entrance of the livery and turned to his angry wife. "Just what I said. He's already paid for your mending and washing."

Marching across the yard, she held out her hand and demanded the money. "I worked for that money, it's MINE!" she shrieked.

"No. It's ours and I'll decide what to do with it," he replied calmly.

"Since when?" she shouted.

"Since now," he said firmly.

Loretta stood speechless as her husband turned his back to her and walked into the stables. She stamped her foot angrily and shook her fists. She cursed him under her breath.

"We'll just see about that!" she muttered as she stalked back to the house.

Several hours later, Loretta was hanging more laundry on the line. She turned abruptly when she spied the stranger standing by the livery corral.

"Ma'am," he said, tipping his hat in her direction. "I told your husband I would be by this afternoon for my clothes."

Loretta watched him light a cigarette. He leaned against the fence as if he didn't have a care in the world.

"Yes he did," she said, picking up the neat pile of clothes she had laid out in a separate basket. "That will be fifty cents," she requested.

When he didn't make any move to pay her, she added, "I also mended your shirt. I don't think you'll find any fault with my sewing."

The stranger picked up the previously torn shirt from the pile and examined it carefully. He nodded his approval.

"Fifty cents," she repeated, holding out her hand.

"I've already paid your husband as I'm sure he told you," the stranger said, glaring at her.

Loretta flushed hotly. She knew he had already paid for the work and now he knew she was trying to cheat him.

With that readymade dress and bonnet becoming a faded dream, Loretta stamped her foot and cursed loudly. "Damn that husband of mine!"

"Carl, I believe your wife has something she'd like for you to hear," the gambler said over his shoulder.

Carl stepped out from the livery. Loretta glared at both men.

"Damn it Carl. I want my money!" she shouted.

"Madam, I have already asked you once to stop swearing," the stranger said, his stern voice capturing Loretta's complete attention.

"Well I don't give a..." Loretta retorted but was cut off.

"LORETTA! SHUT YOUR MOUTH!" Carl barked.

His wife was taken aback and gaped openly at his authoritativeness.

"Come with me," he commanded, taking a firm hold of her upper arm.

Loretta was so shocked by his tone that she let him lead her to the backside of their house without protest. He didn't stop until they were standing next to the neatly stacked row of firewood.

"You will watch your tongue from now on," Carl said sternly. "And I'll not allow any more cursing!"

The stranger leaned alongside of the house and lit another cigarette. He watched and listened as Carl laid down the law to his shrew of a wife about their finances. With each word Carl spoke, he was regaining his self-respect and confidence. The stranger stared on as Carl bent his wife over the ricks of firewood and raised her skirt.

With her plump white ass exposed, Carl unbuckled his belt and doubled it in his hand. He hesitated for a moment. The stranger took a long drag on his cigarette and reminded Carl of her disrespect and that she had tried to cheat him. With no further encouragement, Carl's leather belt made contact with his wife's behind.

"Things are gonna change around here," Carl instructed. "I've had all the browbeating from you I'm gonna take," he said as he thrashed his wife's bare ass, leaving large welts across each cheek.

"Who do you think you are?" Loretta asked bitterly.

"I'm your husband and I'm gonna curb that sharp tongue of yours if it's the last thing I do!" Carl shouted as he gave her another lash with his belt.

"OOOHHH...you're killing me!" she screamed.

Her sobs and pleadings had no effect as Carl continued to punish her. Her pale globes were on their way to turning a deep red when the stranger picked up his clean laundry and went to mount his horse.

A grin appeared on the gambler's face as he urged his horse into a gallop. Carl was giving his wife and the town an earful. The unmistakable "thwack" of the belt as it struck naked flesh echoed down the street. Loretta's cries of remorse and promise to become obedient and respectful carried to the stranger's ears as he left town.

REAL
SPANKING

BY C. C. BARRETT

"I told you it needs to go into our CHECKING ACCOUNT! Why don't you listen to ME?" Catlin shouted at her husband, Tony.

Tony looked at the bank teller, clearly embarrassed by the scene his wife was making. Several other customers looked over. The teller handling the drive-thru turned to give her co-worker and Tony a sympathetic sigh.

"Why do I have to explain this over and over," Catlin continued on snidely.

"Sorry about the mix up." Tony apologized to the patient teller.

The bank employee quickly made the deposit and gave Tony a receipt.

"Thank you and have a nice day," the girl behind the counter said as Catlin turned away.

"Thank you," Tony replied, taking a firm grasp of his wife's hand and leading her to the nearest exit.

"Where are we going?" Catlin asked as he opened the door to their car. "We've still got a few errands to run."

"Those will have to wait," Tony said, staring at his wife.

"But...but," she responded.

"Don't ever talk to me like that again," he said through clenched teeth.

Catlin knew better than to say anything more. She understood that her outburst was uncalled for.

"You embarrassed me...and YOURSELF," he continued to rebuke her as he started the car.

Catlin could think of a hundred excuses, but the only words she spoke were "I'm sorry".

"You WILL be," Tony replied as he stepped on the accelerator, a little bit harder than usual.

It was a silent ride home as Catlin contemplated what he meant by his ominous words. Is he really going to give me a punishment spanking for this, she wondered.

Tony sped through traffic, careful not to run any red lights. Catlin could see he was exceeding the speed limit but only by a few miles per hour. Somehow the ride home seemed longer as they drove on in silence. She could feel his anger seething from him as he watched the road, careful not to look in her direction.

Catlin's stomach began to quiver with anticipation. Her husband had never spanked her for real before. She had mixed emotions and spent the time riding home trying to figure them out.

On the one hand I deserve to be chastised for speaking to my husband so nastily, she thought. He didn't deserve to be treated that way. He was only trying to help make my life easier by making the deposit, she realized.

On the other hand, she knew a spanking would hurt and her husband had the strength to make it last as long as he deemed necessary for her to learn a lesson. Her only real fear was that he would spank her while he was so outraged.

When they arrived at the house, two puppies greeted them at the door. Luckily for her, they hadn't torn up anything while she and Tony were out. Misbehaving puppies would only add to her husband's irritation.

Tony asked her to prepare supper while he performed a few chores around the house. Catlin watched him go out to the garage, wondering if he was still cross.

While she was cleaning up after dinner, she felt her husband's arms circle around her waist. She could feel his warm breath on her ear.

"I love you," he said giving her a hug from behind.

"I love you too. And I'm really sorry about what I said," she replied as she turned in his arms to face him.

"I know you are sweetheart. And I'll try not to be too harsh when I remember this the next time I spank you," Tony said softly.

The words "next time" rang in her head. So he isn't going to spank me for my misbehavior and disrespectfulness after all, she thought disappointedly. Although she'd been anxious about the possibility of a real spanking, it didn't make her feel any better.

They watched television as usual and went to bed. Catlin still felt guilty about how she had treated Tony.

"I love you and I'm really, really sorry," she said before kissing him goodnight.

"I know, and I love you too," he replied, kissing her on the lips.

He rolled over and turned off the light.

***

The next morning, Catlin woke to the touch of her husband's warm hands caressing her back and shoulders.

When he knew she was awake, he ran his fingers through her hair and gently tugged her close to him. His cock was rock hard and he wanted her to give him the release he'd been dreaming about. With his fingers still laced in her hair, he urged her face toward his cock. Catlin saw his erection and immediately knew what Tony wanted.

Repositioning herself, she got on her knees and leaned over his leg. Putting one hand on the mattress to support her upper body, she used her other hand to grasp his throbbing dick. Slowly she took him in her mouth. A soft groan escaped his lips as she smiled to herself. Using her hand as an extension of her mouth, she squeezed his cock and sucked on his engorged member. His dick slid between her lips, in and out of her moist mouth. Her teeth gently scraped against the head and shaft. He humped at her face as his climax built.

"Suck harder, that's it baby," he instructed. "Keep going, I'm gonna cum. Let it spew on your face," he moaned.

Tony massaged Catlin's scalp as his dick pulsated, his hot load sprayed on her cheek and chin, dripping onto her tits as she sat up on her knees. She wiped his cum from her tits and face, licking each finger clean.

They lay together for several minutes. Catlin looked up into her husband's eyes and knew what she had to ask.

"What is it?" he asked, puzzled by her nervous expression.

"Are you going to spank me for what I did yesterday?" she asked, almost in a whisper.

Tony didn't say anything for a long time while Catlin waited with bated breath.

"Is that what you need?" he finally asked.

Catlin didn't respond right away. Is it what I NEED, she wondered. She always had a hard time asking for a spanking. But this time she was asking for a REAL spanking, for punishment. Catlin didn't want to feel the pain of the paddle he would use, although she knew she deserved it.

"Yes, I do," she finally whispered.

"Do you want me to do it now or before bedtime?" he asked.

All these questions, she wanted to scream. Isn't it enough that I had to ask to be punished, she thought. With another decision to make, her mind began to turn. Put the spanking off verses get it over with. She weighed her options. If she put it off, she might dread what was to come all day long and even be tempted to plead for mercy. And worse still, he might actually grant her that mercy. But to get it over with meant she would probably have to endure a sore bottom most of the day.

"Now," she finally said through trembling lips.

"Okay. Get on your knees, bottom up," he said matter-of-factly.

Catlin positioned herself as she'd done so many times before only this time it was for a very REAL spanking. During this spanking she knew she would have no control, no safe word would save her.

I can't believe I asked for this, she thought as she laid her head down on the mattress, presenting her exposed cheeks to her husband. Her face reddened with humiliation and guilt as her bare ass stuck up in the air.

She didn't bother to look at what he pulled out of the spanking drawer. There were numerous implements for him to choose from that had collected over time. Somehow she knew he would choose the paddle he recently made her for Christmas. She remembered complaining about how much it hurt when he first tried it out on her.

"Ten," he said as he drew his arm back.

Catlin cringed into her pillow and waited for the first whack.

CRACK! The sound and pain simultaneously hit her. She felt the wood strike across both cheeks.

"One," he said.

"OHHHH," she whined as the pain seared her flesh.

The next whack was in the same spot. It soon became clear to Catlin that her husband intended to deliver each strike to the same place on her backside. By number six, her ass changed from bright pink to white as the 3/4 inch thick board struck her flesh over and over.

"Seven," Tony said, bringing the paddle down

evenly across both cheeks.

Catlin began to squirm and cry into her pillow. I can't take any more, her mind screamed. She tried to remain still. Only a few more, she counted in her head as the next swats were given.

"I'm sorry," she cried through her pillow.

"Ten," Tony finally counted the last stroke of the paddle.

"I'm sorry," she said again, this time louder, hoping her husband would hear her. She breathed a sigh of relief that it was over. Tony walked back to the drawer and Catlin could hear him put the paddle down.

She was surprised when he came back to stand next to the bed and didn't offer her comfort. Instead he held a leather strap he'd purchase only a few days ago.

"I don't think you're sorry enough," he said as he drew back with the double thick leather.

The two inch rawhide struck her right ass cheek and then quickly struck her left. He alternated between bouncing globes until he reached twelve licks.

Catlin wept into her pillow as the leather stung the fleshy part of her bottom. Relief swept over her when he walked toward the drawer to put the strap away.

She felt his warm loving hands caress her back. Catlin continued to sniffle into the pillow a little longer. She felt his weight lift off the mattress.

Lying flat on her stomach, she turned her head. Catlin was confused when he picked up the yard stick and brought it back to the bed. Before she could protest, she felt three hard smacks of the wooden stick across her throbbing ass.

"OOHH, OOOHHH," she cried, feeling the burn of her punishment.

"Okay. It's over. I'm through spanking you," Tony said. "Unless you want to continue to lay there, in which case I'm sure I can find something else to use, maybe the cane."

Catlin quickly got off the bed and was about to go into the bathroom. She looked at the clock and realized she only had an hour to get ready for work. Tony sat on the edge of the mattress and grabbed both her hands. He made her stand in front of him as he looked up into her face.

"How many did I give you?" he asked.

"Twenty-five," she said meekly.

"I love you and I forgive you. Do you feel better now?" he asked.

She hugged him tightly and nodded her head.

"I love you too. I'm sorry," she whispered into his ear.

Stopping in front of the bathroom mirror, Catlin examined her bottom. The paddle and yard stick left a large glowing area near her sit spot. The leather strap strikes were clearly defined by the puffy pink rectangular marks on her fanny. Her whole bottom felt warm to the touch. She rubbed her sore backside before stepping into the warm shower.

"Want me to wash your back?" he asked.

NOT ALONE

BY C. C. BARRETT

Tammy sat by her mother's bedside, listening to her ragged breathing. The doctor said his patient, Deloris Holliday, didn't have much longer to live. The nurse had left the room, leaving them alone.

"Tammy...I...must tell you..." Deloris said between gasps.

"Don't try to talk," Tammy said, holding the woman's hand gently.

"But I must..." her mother said in earnest. "It's about your father..."

Tammy didn't want her mother to overexert herself but Deloris had never mentioned her father.

Every time Tammy asked about him, her mother would always change the subject.

Leaning in closer, Tammy squeezed her mother's hand.

"His name…his name is…" Deloris began.

"Mommy…you don't have to," Tammy replied, knowing how hard it must be for her mother to speak of someone she obviously wanted to forget.

"Had…en…His name is Thomas…Haden," Deloris croaked. "Spelled like…your middle…name," she finished with an exhausted breath.

Deloris's breathing became more labored. Tammy pushed the button to summon the nurse.

"Wait…wait," her mother whispered. "You…must know…more. He lives in Logg…Hollow…Go to him…when I'm…gone…" Deloris closed her eyes as her breathing became more difficult.

"Logg Hollow?" Tammy couldn't believe her father lived only thirty miles away from where she'd grown up.

"Mommy? MOMMY!" Tammy shook her mother and pressed the nurse's button urgently.

***

Three weeks after her mother's funeral, Tammy was sitting in the middle of Deloris's bedroom. She had separated most of her mother's clothes. Setting aside a pile to be given to charity, all that remained were old pictures and a small stuffed pig she found in the back of her mother's closet.

Most of the pictures were of Tammy when she was growing up. They never had much money but her mother always took at least one picture at every birthday.

Just as she was about to add the little pink toy to the charity pile, she stopped. There wasn't anything familiar about the pig at all. Thinking it strange, Tammy began looking through her baby pictures. As she flipped through each one, she looked to see if the small stuffed animal was among the surroundings. Not finding it in any of the pictures, Tammy took a closer look at the toy.

The pink material had faded, she could tell as she lifted one of the little ears. It wasn't an expensive toy, something one would expect to win at a carnival. As she turned it over in her hand, Tammy noticed that the underbelly had been re-sewn by hand. It probably got torn and mommy repaired it, Tammy thought. But it still puzzled her why she couldn't remember the pig as a child. Her mother hadn't saved any of her other stuffed animals except for a favorite teddy bear.

"Why save this?" Tammy asked aloud.

***

"You stay put Deloris Holliday," Thomas said. "I'm going to win you something if it takes all night!"

"Come on Thomas, I want to ride the Ferris wheel," she complained. "If you don't come with me,

I'll just have to find someone who will," she threatened in a singsong voice.

"Don't even think about it," he laughed before taking aim and releasing the baseball.

"And why would you care if I do find someone else?" she asked teasingly.

"Don't test me…" he warned.

Deloris giggled and ran off to get in line to ride the Ferris wheel.

Several minutes later, with prize in hand, Thomas went in search of Deloris. He finally found her on the carnival ride with a man he'd never seen before. Their car was stopped near the top as they sat together. Deloris squealed as the man began to rock the seat. They were sitting too close and the man had his arm draped casually around her shoulders.

Thomas waited impatiently for the car to descend and for its passengers to get off. He wasted no time in marching up to Deloris and grabbing her by the hand. Tugging her along behind him, he announced that he was going to take her home.

"But it's early," she complained, refusing to get into his car.

Opening the door for her, he ushered her into the passenger's seat of his Bel Air. Without another word, he threw the prize onto the back seat and started the engine.

"See the fun is just starting…more people are arriving," she pointed out as several cars were trying to find parking spaces in the field next to the carnival.

Turning off the engine, he turned and stared at Deloris.

"Do you have any idea how angry I am right now?" he asked.

"I just went for a ride…" she began.

"With some man you don't even know!" he finished for her.

"I do so. His name is Matthew and he asked if he could take me home," she spouted.

"And what did you say?" he asked, glaring at her.

"I said I'd THINK about it!" she replied haughtily.

Without another word, Thomas got out of the car. He came around to Deloris's side and opened the door with a tug. She got out in a huff, ready to give her boyfriend a piece of her mind. But before she could open her mouth, he bent her over the trunk of his car and began swatting her fanny. Her poodle skirt didn't offer much protection as he swatted harder and harder. Deloris could see people, who were on their way toward the carnival, stopping to watch as Thomas reddened her backside.

"Ouch! OUCH!" Deloris cried out as her bottom began to burn with his continued spanks.

A few chuckles from some of the spectators added to Deloris's humiliation.

With her pride hurt almost as much as her derriere, she refused to speak to Thomas as he drove her home.

Thomas berated himself for losing his temper and regretted spanking his girlfriend in public. He knew he should have waited until they were alone, down by Miller's pond where no one would see them. He cursed his timing as well, hoping they could go there like they did last week.

As he continued to drive along with Deloris pouting beside him, his thoughts drifted back to that night at the secluded spot. He and Deloris had decided to go skinny dipping after leaving the ice cream shop. It was a hot and humid night with a full moon. He hadn't planned on things going as far as they had but one thing led to another. Before each of them knew it, they were both lying naked on a blanket by the water's edge. Her nipples were hard, stimulated by the cool spring water. The sight of her perfectly formed body gave him a hardon like no wet dream he'd ever had before. She never spoke a word of protest when his hand cupped her firm breast. Her eyes seemed bluer as they stared at him longingly. His other hand moved to the juncture of her legs, parting them with a nudge. A soft moan escaped her lips as his finger moved over her feminine folds. Her eyes never wavered from his as he spread her legs farther apart. Her body arched up to meet his hand as he continued to rub her clit. His dick throbbed as it pressed against her thigh.

With both hands, she reached up and pulled his face closer to her own. He kissed her, slowly at first, and then positioned himself between her legs. His hands found her naked backside and kneaded her ass cheeks. A moan escaped her lips as the head of his cock rubbed her clit. Their kiss turned urgent. At almost the same time, her body arched up to meet his thrusting member. He plunged inside of her for the first time. A tear slid down her face but he was oblivious. His body thrust in rhythm to his passionately beating heart. With both hands, he squeezed her ass, sending her into an orgasmic spin. Pressing her body to him, he filled her with his seed.

The remembrance of their love making made Thomas's cock grow hard as he continued to drive. He glanced in Deloris's direction but she remained stiff as she stared out the window. He reached behind him and grabbed the stuffed prize from the backseat.

"I won this for you," he said gently, placing the little pig in her lap.

Deloris turned and with tears brimming in her eyes, replied softly, "You spanked me and humiliated me in front of all those people."

"I'm not sorry I spanked you," Thomas replied. "But I am sorry people saw it," he said sincerely.

They rode in silence for a few more miles. As they came to the turn off toward Miller's pond, Thomas pulled over; wanting to recapture the magic they shared last week.

"No, take me home," Deloris said tightly, reading his intentions correctly.

With a heavy sigh, Thomas pulled back onto the main road. A few minutes later, he stopped in the driveway of her parents' house. Deloris didn't wait for him to come around to open her door. She bolted from the seat.

Through the open window she yelled at him. "I hate you Thomas Haden! I never want to see you again!"

Hugging the pink pig to her breast she ran into the house. From her bedroom window she watched as Thomas slowly backed out of the driveway. She wished she could take the words back. She didn't realize that she would regret them for the rest of her life.

***

Tammy sat in her car outside the large farm house. A swing set was in the backyard. Identical twin boys, about eight years old, were playing in a tree-house. They were unaware of the tug-of-war going on in Tammy's mind. She didn't know what possessed her to drive to Logg Hollow.

At the local diner, she only had to mention Thomas Haden's name and the waitress directed her a few miles south to the largest dairy farm in the county.

Out of curiosity she drove toward his home. Unbeknownst to her, the road dead ended at the Haden farm.

A knock on her car window startled her. Tammy looked up into a pair of eyes that matched her own. She was flustered and didn't know what to do.

Thomas had seen the car stop in front of the house. He didn't think much of it since drivers, unfamiliar with the area, occasionally mistaken his long driveway for Route 354.

When the car didn't move for several minutes and knowing his boys were only a few yards away playing, he decided to check it out.

Thomas opened Tammy's door for her. "Are you lost? Can I help you?" he asked.

"Who is she?" the twins hollered down from their tree-house.

Seeing the distressed look on Tammy's face, Thomas yelled up at his boys, "Andy, Alex, you two go on into the house and wash up for supper."

"Are you okay?" Thomas asked, turning back to Tammy with concern.

But before Tammy could say anything, a lovely brunette, about her mother's age, came out onto the porch. Behind her was a teenage girl, maybe a year younger than Tammy.

"Is everything alright Thomas?" the lady asked.

"I...I...I'm sorry. I shouldn't have come," Tammy said uncomfortably, glancing away from Thomas's wife and daughter.

"Are you looking for someone?" Thomas asked.

"I should go," she said, about to climb back into her car.

"No wait, please," Thomas said as his concern deepened.

"Everything's fine Nora. You and Stacy go back inside," he shouted up to the front porch.

"You look familiar. What's your father's name?" he asked, trying to place her around town.

Tammy laughed nervously at his question. When she drove to Logg Hollow, she never envisioned actually seeing her father, let alone talking to him.

"Thomas Haden," she said softly, looking down at her hands as they twisted nervously together.

"Yes, I'm Thomas Haden," he said, confused.

"No. That's the answer to your question," she replied hesitantly before looking up at her father.

It took a moment for what she had said to sink in. Suddenly he understood why she looked so familiar. A picture of Deloris popped into his head but there was something different about this girl. His brows shot up in disbelief as he realized his own eyes were staring back up at him.

"Daddy, Mom said to tell you…" Stacy called from the porch.

"Not now Stacy!" he said sternly, not wanting to take his eyes off of Tammy.

Stacy shrugged her shoulders and went back into the house, letting the screen door close with a loud bang.

"I'm Tammy. My mother was…"

"Deloris," they both said at the same time.

"That's right. Deloris Holliday was my mother," Tammy looked back down as tears began to pool in her eyes at the remembrance of her recently departed mother.

"Was?" Thomas asked, suddenly very aware of Tammy's use of the past tense.

"Yes. She passed away a few weeks ago. The doctors said she had a bad heart," Tammy explained.

"I...I didn't know. I'm sorry," Thomas said sadly.

"Just before she died she told me who you were and where you lived," she said as tears streamed down her face.

Tammy looked toward the house. Several pairs of eyes were watching them from the big bay window.

"I shouldn't have come. You have a family and...and I should probably go," she said hurriedly.

"No wait. Please don't go. I never knew about you," he said, choking up a bit.

Tammy hesitated. She didn't really want to leave; her only living relative was standing before her. She had so many questions, one which was now answered. Thomas never knew Deloris was pregnant; her father hadn't abandoned her as she had imagined.

"Please stay. I want you to meet your new family," Thomas said, putting his arm around her shoulders and walking her toward the farm house.

***

"Tammy, Stacy! I need your help in the kitchen," Nora hollered up the stairs.

The girls had been inseparable since Tammy came to live with them. It took a few adjustments.

Nora resented Tammy from the onset, refusing to accept Thomas's decision to take in his child by Deloris, his first love.

"Tammy is 19 years old," Nora argued.

Several closely timed trips to the barn and a very sore backside had Nora accepting Tammy's presence in their lives before the movers had arrived.

They still didn't always get along, especially when Nora was convinced that Tammy was being a bad influence on Stacy. Her daughter had begun to ignore her chores, becoming disrespectful and defiant lately.

Even now, when the two girls were expected to help with the housework, they were upstairs painting their nails and listening to the radio too loudly.

Every time Nora complained, Thomas would remind her, usually by way of his belt, that it had only been a few months since Tammy had come into their lives. He had said they all just needed time to adjust.

"It's time Tammy adjusts to US!" Nora grumbled as she marched to the foot of the stairs.

"STACY! TAMMY! COME DOWN HERE RIGHT NOW!" Nora yelled.

"Okay, Okay!" Stacy yelled back down.

Nora could hear their giggles. "You'd think they were 12 instead of 18 and 19," she murmured irritably.

"You yelled?" Stacy asked belligerently, jumping the last two steps down the stairs.

"I asked you loud enough for you to hear me," her mother corrected.

"What do you want?" Stacy rolled her eyes. Tammy giggled as if the two shared a private joke.

"I want BOTH of you to do your share around here," Nora said angrily.

"WHAT, what do you want us to do?" Stacy asked, pretending she didn't know the chores her mother was alluding to.

"The two of you were to clean this kitchen after lunch and look! The dirty dishes are still in the sink!" Nora ranted.

"We've been busy," Tammy said lamely, coming down the stairs a bit more slowly.

"And YOU!" Nora rounded on Tammy. "I don't like the way you've been influencing Stacy! Since you got here..."Nora was cut off.

"NORA!" a deep male voice barked.

All three women turned to see Thomas standing in the doorway. None of them knew how long he had been listening to them.

"Thomas, I'm sorry, it's just..." Nora tried to explain her outburst.

"We'll talk about it...later and not HERE," he said firmly, sending her a clear message.

Nora shuddered when she thought of what was in store for her after the children were asleep. She knew she would be sleeping on her stomach tonight when he finished disciplining her.

***

After supper, Thomas sent the twins outside to play. Nora, Stacy and Tammy remained at the table at Thomas's request.

"First I want to say how happy I am that Tammy is here with us," he began.

Tammy gave him a huge smile. Although they had only met a few months before, she had grown to adore her father.

"But, with that said…" Thomas went on. "You girls haven't been doing your chores."

His reproachful tone had both girls looking down at the table. A smirk appeared on Nora's face.

"I'm very disappointed in the three of you," he said disdainfully, causing Nora's smirk to disappear immediately.

Stacy's eyes filled with tears as she looked toward her father.

"Daddy I'm sorry," Stacy said, clearly upset.

"Thomas, I'm sorry too," Nora echoed nervously.

"Didn't I ask you girls to sterilize the milking hoses yesterday?" he asked, looking at Stacy and Tammy.

"Yes sir," Stacy replied timidly.

Tammy bashfully nodded her head in an affirmative manner.

"Did you do it?" he asked, knowing full well they hadn't.

"No sir," his youngest daughter said dejectedly.

Tammy shook her head from side to side, afraid to meet her father's eyes.

"You both disobeyed me," Thomas said, with disappointment in his eyes.

"Daddy, I'm sorry," Stacy appealed to him immediately.

"Both of you are to go upstairs and go to bed. Tomorrow morning before breakfast, while you're still in your nightgowns, I want you girls to meet me in the barn," Thomas said firmly.

"Daddy please," Stacy begged.

"Go upstairs, now," he said curtly, defying any argument.

Tammy followed Stacy to the bedroom they shared. Stacy flung herself onto her bed and cried into the pillow.

She imagined that their father is going to make them clean the milk hoses in the morning before breakfast and even before getting dressed. It isn't something to get so upset about, she thought, puzzled by her half-sister's reaction.

"I wish he'd just get it over with!" Stacy's voice was muffled by the pillow.

"What? Cleaning dumb old hoses?" Tammy asked, irritated by Stacy's dramatics.

"No," Stacy said, turning her head to face her sister. "The whipping we're going to get tomorrow morning," she snapped.

"Whipping? What are you talking about?" Tammy's voice cracked.

"Daddy is going to spank us for disobeying him," Stacy clarified through her tears.

"He can't! I'm 19 and you're 18!" Tammy exclaimed, not believing her ears.

"Age doesn't matter to Daddy. He even spanks Mom," Stacy explained.

"You can't be serious!" Tammy's heart was now beating a mile a minute.

"Yes he does. He thinks we're all asleep but I've heard them down at the barn," Stacy said.

More than nervous, Tammy was now scared. She'd never been spanked in her entire life.

"What...what will happen?" Alarm and curiosity made Tammy ask.

Stacy sat up on the bed. She took a few deep breaths and wiped the tears from her eyes.

"Well...first he talks to us...you know. He asks us why we are about to be spanked," Stacy tried to keep the tremor from her voice as she recounted what the girls could expect in the morning.

"Then he'll make us raise our nightgowns. Don't bother wearing underwear," Stacy cautioned. "Daddy will only make you pull them down to your ankles."

Tammy's heart was beating so fast she clutched her chest.

Stacy continued, "He'll probably talk some more and then he'll take off his belt..."

"What's he going to do with his belt?" Tammy asked fearfully.

"He'll make you bend over and grab the rail; you know where the cows stick their heads through, except there won't be any cows in the barn yet," Stacy continued.

"Why do we have to hold onto the rail?" her sister asked.

"To keep from reaching behind; Daddy will start the whipping over if you try to reach behind to protect yourself," Stacy said with a warning tone.

"Will it hurt?" Tammy asked, her voice trembling.

"A wh...whole bunch," Stacy assured her, with a nervous tremble in her voice.

"Maybe he won't...I mean this is my first time disobeying him..." Tammy tried to convince herself.

Stacy shook her head and grimaced. "He'll make you bare your bottom right alongside of mine," she predicted.

"Turn off the light and go to sleep," Thomas said tersely as he passed their bedroom door.

"Yes sir," the girls said in unison.

Tammy pulled the covers up to her chin. She couldn't imagine that the same man she'd grown to love and admire would actually spank her bare bottom with his belt. I'm too old for that, she tried to rationalize.

"You're just trying to scare me," Tammy whispered to Stacy, trying to drive back her own fear.

"No I'm not," Stacy hissed back, tears clouding her eyes. "You'll see tomorrow," she replied ominously before rolling over to face the wall.

It was after ten o'clock and Tammy was still awake. The house was quiet when she heard Nora and her father descend the stairs and go out the back door.

97

After looking over to see if Stacy was asleep, she crept from her bed and peered out the bedroom window that overlooked the backyard. The barn was about 100 yards away. She watched as Nora, followed by Thomas, went inside. A light was turned on making it easy to see what was happening inside.

Tammy watched as Thomas spoke to his wife. He didn't appear angry but whatever he was saying made Nora begin to cry. To Tammy's horror, she saw Nora pull up her nightgown, exposing her bare butt cheeks.

With one eye on Stacy, Tammy opened the window just a little. She kneeled down and listened through the opening.

When Tammy looked back toward the barn, her step-mother was already reaching forward. She could only envision Nora having a death grip on the railing in front of her. Stacy's warning of how the punishment could start over rang in Tammy's head.

Tammy waited expectantly. It's just as Stacy described, she thought fearfully. She watched as her father drew his doubled belt back and brought it around with such force, the contact could be heard throughout the whole farm. "THWACK!" Tammy heard another lick. Her heart was beating double-time.

"Oh God, no," she whispered, turning suddenly from the sight in the barn and sitting down with her back against the wall. I can't go through that, she thought, quivering in alarm.

Sobs were coming from the barn as the whipping continued. Without success, Tammy pressed her palms to her ears to block out the sound of the belt striking Nora's naked ass. Tammy shut the window quickly and hurried to bed. She closed her eyes, wishing it were only a bad dream.

Fifteen minutes later, Tammy was still wide awake. She heard Nora and Thomas coming in the back door. Tammy got out of bed and grabbed the pink pig, putting it in her robe pocket. She had to talk to her father and didn't want to wait another minute.

Nora gasped in surprise when she saw Tammy standing at the top of the stairs.

"What...what are you doing up?" Nora asked quietly, her face flushing red from embarrassment.

"I need to talk to Daddy," Tammy said, not meeting her step-mother's eyes.

"Nora, it's okay. Go to bed," Thomas said from the bottom of the stairs.

"Tammy, why don't we talk down here so we won't disturb anyone," Thomas suggested.

Tammy moved aside to let Nora pass. She watched her step-mother, with eyes swollen from crying, skirt by. Nora was especially careful not to touch the wall with her backside. Her ass must hurt terribly Tammy thought, remembering Nora's chastisement.

Slowly, Tammy went downstairs. Her father was waiting at the kitchen table.

"Sit down," Thomas said, pointing to the chair opposite his.

"I…I need to…talk to you," Tammy stammered.

"It's late," her father said looking at the clock on the kitchen wall.

"I know but this can't wait," she replied, looking down at the table.

"What is it Tammy?" he asked softly.

"I know…I know what you are going to do to Stacy and me t…tomorrow," Tammy began.

"I figured Stacy would tell you," Thomas said, understanding his daughter's apprehension.

"You…you can't. Please…you just can't," Tammy wrung her hands.

"You disobeyed me. You've been here long enough to know that actions have consequences," Thomas stressed.

"Yes I know…I've seen you spank the twins… but…but they're little and Stacy and I…well…" Tammy couldn't get the sight of Nora's bare backside out of her mind.

"You think you're too old? Is that it?" he asked.

"I…I…this wasn't what I expected when I move in," she said. "I know you haven't known me long but I thought…I thought you loved me," she said as a single tear slid down her face.

"I do," he assured her, reaching for her hand. "It's because I love you that I discipline you when you disobey or do something wrong."

"But I've never been spanked before," she pleaded, trying to make him understand.

"I never told you what happened the night your mother and I broke up, did I?" her father asked.

Tammy shook her head negatively.

Thomas told the story of the night he spanked Deloris by his car at the carnival.

"She said she never wanted to see me again," Thomas said with heavy sadness.

"I don't think she meant it," Tammy said, pulling the pig from her pocket.

A smile crossed Thomas's face when he saw the toy.

"I won this for her...it must have cost me eight games but I finally won it," he said, taking the pig from his daughter.

He turned it over and noticed the spot on its belly that had been re-stitched.

"There's something inside," Thomas said, feeling around.

With his pocket knife, Thomas carefully cut the stitches. As he spread the toy open, a folded picture fell out. He smiled when he recognized it.

"It's of your mom and me...at a dance," he said handing her the picture.

"The two of you looked so happy," Tammy said.

Thomas's eyes watered at her words. "I'm sorry things worked out the way they did," he said, eyeing the picture. "You deserved a father while you were growing up."

"But then you wouldn't have Nora, Stacy or the twins," Tammy replied with a grin.

Thomas laughed, cheered significantly by her wise words.

"Okay young lady. It's pretty late," he said noticing the time.

"Daddy?" Tammy asked. "I understand I need to be punished for disobeying you but...but couldn't you do it now? I mean...why wait until tomorrow morning?"

"It's my decision. The anticipation of a whipping causes a lasting impression and a sore bottom is a good physical reminder. It's time for bed, young lady," he lovingly instructed.

"Yes sir," Tammy said, kissing her father on the cheek before going to bed.

Look for these other titles from C.C. Barrett:

BARE TO DISCIPLINE VOL. 1: M/F Spanking Erotica Discipline Stories, The Apartment Collection Vol.1

BARE TO DISCIPLINE VOL. 2: M/F Spanking Erotica Discipline Stories, The Apartment Collection Vol.2

BRANDED (REVISED EDITION): An Old West Spanking Tale

EXECUTIVE PUNISHMENT

PRISONER OF DISCIPLINE

HALFWAY HOUSE: DISCIPLINED

RAZOR STRAP LEGACY

A SPANKING RICH GOLD RUSH

THE SPANKING ORDER

BARE TO DISCIPLINE VOL. 3: M/F Spanking Erotica Discipline Stories, Vol. 3

THE SEA FLOGGER

BARE TO DISCIPLINE VOL. 4: M/F Spanking Erotica Discipline Stories, Vol. 4

BARE TO DISCIPLINE VOL. 5: M/F Spanking Erotica Discipline Stories, Vol. 5

Made in United States
Troutdale, OR
08/08/2024

21852203R00060